This verse version of
Jack and the Beanstalk
is adapted from the one
written by B. A. T.
that appeared in London
in 1807, published
by J. Harris, corner of
St. Paul's Churchyard

*The assistance of the
Osborne Collection of the Toronto Public Library
is gratefully acknowledged.*

For another Jack

LIBRARY OF CONGRESS CATALOGING IN PUBLICATION DATA

Main entry under title:

The history of Mother Twaddle and the marvelous achievements of her son Jack.

SUMMARY: Jack climbs the great beanstalk that grows from the bean he bought and confronts a giant at the top.

A verse version of Jack and the beanstalk, written by B.A.T. and published in 1807 by J. Harris, London.

[1. Folklore. 2. Fairy tales. 3. Stories in rhyme] I. Galdone, Paul, illus. II. B. A. T. III. T., B. A. IV. Jack and the beanstalk.

PZ8.1.H664   1974   398.2'1'0942   73-9726
ISBN   0-8164-3112-4

The History of
MOTHER TWADDLE
and the Marvelous Achievements,
of her Son
JACK

PAUL GALDONE

The Seabury Press
New York

As Old Mother Twaddle
    Was sweeping her floor,
She found a new sixpence
    Under the door.
And as she surveyed it
    With exquisite pleasure,
She called her son Jack
    To look at her treasure.

"I will comb thee, and wash thee,
  And make thee quite spruce.
Thou shalt go to the fair
  And buy us a goose.
For of all the good things,
  I vow and protest,
A fat, tasty goose
  Is the thing I love best."

When Old Mother Twaddle
Had sent Jack to the fair,
She hastened with onions
And sage to prepare
A savory stuffing
For the delicate treat,
And thought with what glee
Of the tidbits she'd eat.

When Jack reached the fair
    And round him was staring
A peddler cried out,
    "Buy this bean for a farthing.
It possesses such virtues
    That sure as a gun,
Tomorrow it will grow
    Near as high as the sun!"

Jack bought it for sixpence
    Then went to his Mother,
Who at sight of the bean
    Made a terrible pother.
She gave him a scolding
    And slapped both his hands,
For having presumed
    Not to mind her commands.

Jack went to the garden
  And took up his spade,
Then put the rare bean
  In the hole he had made,
Expecting to find
  This great wonder of wonders
As tall as a tree
  To make up for his blunders.

ext morning Jack rose
 To view the large bean,
When to his surprise,
 E'en the top was not seen!
It made a long ladder
 As strong as a rope,
And Jack soon climbed on high
 Full of joy and of hope.

He knocked at the door
   Of a very grand place;
A damsel came to it
   With a cap all of lace.
"Oh! Pray go from hence!"
   Cried this maid in a fright,
"For a giant lives here,
   And he'll eat you this night!"

Jack begged to come in
     With so winning an air
That she promised to hide him
     And pointed out where.
He no sooner had hidden
     Than the door opened wide,
And in stalked the Giant
     With a very long stride.

Then the Monster roared out,
  "Fe, fi, fo, fan!
I smell the breath
  Of an Englishman!
If he be alive,
  Or if he be dead,
I'll grind his bones
  To make my bread!"

"Oh wait, my dear Giant,
    First drink some strong wine,
Then on that dainty
    You may afterwards dine."
He seized a large cup
    And tippled so deep,
Then he tumbled down flat
    And fell fast asleep.

Soon as Jack saw him fall,
He crept from the bed,
Then snatched a large knife
And chopped off his head.
Thus he killed this great man,
As he loudly did snore,
And never again
Was a Giant seen more.

Jack sent for his Mother
     To come up and dine,
With a promise of goose
     And a bottle of wine.
And as she did eat it
     With excessive delight,
She approved of his bargain
     And said he'd done right.

Jack sent for a parson,
　　As he had a great mind
To marry the damsel,
　　Who was willing and kind.
The Parson came soon
　　And made her Jack's Wife,
And they lived very happy
　　To the end of their life.

Here Jack, and his Wife,
  And his Mother are seen
All dancing a jig
  Round the wonderful bean.